A Bee on a Lark

Written by Helen Baugh
Illustrated by Keri Green

Collins

A bee on a lark,

a bug on a shark,

3

a lark on a fox,

a shark on a box.

A fox in a jeep,

a box on a sheep,

a jeep on a goat,

a sheep in a boat.

Titter, totter,

teeter, boom!

Get in the rocket ...

off they zoom!

Lark and shark

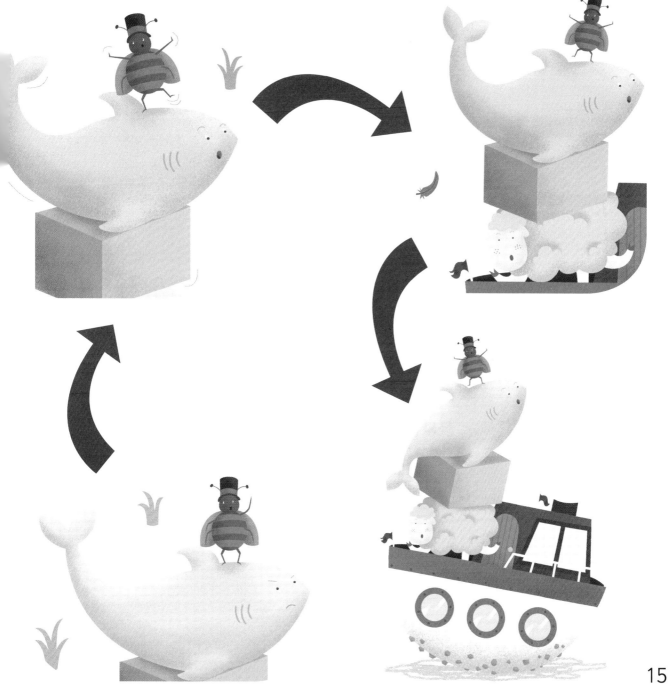

After reading

Letters and Sounds: Phase 3

Word count: 54

Focus phonemes: /ar/ /oa/ /ee/ /er/ /oo/ /tt/ tt

Common exception words: the, they

Curriculum links: Understanding the World: The World

Early learning goals: Listening and attention: listen to stories, accurately anticipating key events and respond to what is heard with relevant comments, questions or actions; Understanding: answer 'how' and 'why' questions about experiences and in response to stories or events; Reading: read and understand simple sentences; use phonic knowledge to decode regular words and read them aloud accurately; read some common irregular words

Developing fluency

- Your child may enjoy hearing you read the story.
- Look at the story map on pages 14 and 15. Ask your child to retell the story in their own words.

Phonic practice

- Look at the words **shark** and **lark** together on pages 2 and 3. Ask your child if they notice anything about these two words. (*They rhyme.*)
- Ask your child to sound talk and blend each word.
- Can they tell you which letter sound is the same in the two words? Which letters are different?
- Can they think of any other words that rhyme with **shark** and **lark**? (e.g. *bark, park, dark*)
- Do the same for the following pairs of words:

  sheep / jeep

  goat / boat

  boom / zoom